**NFL TEAM STORIES**

*The Story of the*

# CLEVELAND BROWNS

By Diane Bailey

**Kaleidoscope**
Minneapolis, MN

## The Quest for Discovery Never Ends

...................................................

This edition first published in 2021 by Kaleidoscope Publishing, Inc.

No part of this publication may be reproduced in whole or in part without written permission of the publisher.

For information regarding permission, write to
Kaleidoscope Publishing, Inc.
6012 Blue Circle Drive
Minnetonka, MN 55343

Library of Congress Control Number
2020933806

ISBN
978-1-64519-225-1 (library bound)
978-1-64519-293-0 (ebook)

Text copyright © 2021 by Kaleidoscope Publishing, Inc. All-Star Sports, Bigfoot Books, and associated logos are trademarks and/or registered trademarks of Kaleidoscope Publishing, Inc.

Printed in the United States of America.

FIND ME IF YOU CAN!

Bigfoot lurks within one of the images in this book. It's up to you to find him!

# TABLE OF CONTENTS

Kickoff!...................................................................... 4

**Chapter 1:** Browns History ................................................ 6

**Chapter 2:** Browns All-Time Greats ............................... 16

**Chapter 3:** Browns Superstars ........................................ 22

Beyond the Book........................................................ 28
Research Ninja............................................................ 29
Further Resources ..................................................... 30
Glossary ...................................................................... 31
Index ........................................................................... 32
Photo Credits ............................................................. 32
About the Author...................................................... 32

# KICKOFF!

**W**oof! Woof! Cleveland Browns fans are barking like dogs. Sometimes the players bark back! It gets everyone excited! Why all the barking? Part of Cleveland's stadium is called the "Dawg Pound." **Loyal** fans sit here. They chant when the Browns start a big play. "Here we go, Brownies, here we go!" Want to know more?

Here we go!

# Chapter 1
# Browns History

The Cleveland Browns started in 1946. They were in the All-America Football Conference (AAFC). They were named for their coach, Paul Brown. The Browns won their first game, 44-0! Quarterback Otto Graham led the team. He could always find his best pass receivers. Mac Speedie was one. He lived up to his name. He was *fast*! Dante Lavelli came through with tough catches. The Browns won their league championship title for the next four years.

## SPORTS PIONEERS

In the 1940s, most sports teams did not allow African American players. Paul Brown did not care about that. He just wanted good football players! In 1946, he signed two African Americans, Marion Motley and Bill Willis. The Browns helped open up pro sports to all players.

**FUN FACT**
Marion Motley led the NFL in rushing in 1950.

**FUN FACT**

The San Francisco 49ers and Baltimore Colts also moved over from the AAFC.

In 1950, the AAFC stopped playing. The Browns joined the NFL that year. Cleveland played the Los Angeles Rams for the NFL title. With 28 seconds left, the Browns were down by one point. Lou Groza kicked a field goal to give Cleveland the win. After that, they kept on winning. Cleveland took home three NFL championships in the 1950s! They won again in 1964.

The Browns struggled in the 1970s and 1980s. They came close in some playoff games. Still, they could not make it to the Super Bowl. One bright spot came in 1989. They played the Pittsburgh Steelers, one of their main **rivals**. The Browns stomped the Steelers, 51-0! That is Pittsburgh's worst loss ever.

Tim Manoa rumbled for the Browns in the 1980s.

In 1996, the Browns' owner decided to move the team to Baltimore, Maryland. Browns fans were angry! They had been loyal for years. In the end, only the players left. The "Browns" name stayed with Cleveland. The NFL gave Cleveland another Browns team. In 1999, the Browns were back on the field.

The new team was not very good. Many of the players were **rookies**. Some had been cut from other teams. They all had to learn to work together. They had a lot of catching up to do!

*Cleveland QB Tim Couch*

Karim Abdul-Jabbar went up and over for a TD in 1999.

The Browns went to the playoffs in 2002. By 2016 they were going downhill, though. In 2016 and 2017, they only won one game out of 32! The Browns signed some top players for the 2019 season. Unfortunately, the team did not do as well as people hoped. They finished with a 6-10 record. The fans still love their "Brownies." They believe they can turn things around!

*Team mascot "Brownie" poses with Browns fans.*

# TIMELINE OF THE CLEVELAND BROWNS

**1946**

1946: The Browns win the first of four straight AAFC titles.

**1950**

1950: The Browns join the NFL and win the league championship in their first year.

**1964**

1964: Cleveland takes home another NFL championship.

**1980**

1980: The Browns win their division championship. Several last-minute wins make it an exciting season.

**1984**

1984: The Browns' defense describes itself as "dogs." Fans love it and start to call a section of the bleachers the "Dawg Pound."

**1999**

1999: After three years off, the new Cleveland Browns begin playing again.

**2017**

2017: A winless season gives Cleveland the first pick in the NFL draft. They select quarterback Baker Mayfield.

# PROVE IT!

Otto Graham (center) and Paul Brown (right) after the big 1950 win.

In their early years, the Cleveland Browns beat almost everyone. They won the AAFC championship every year from 1946 to 1949. Then the Browns joined the NFL. A lot of people thought the NFL was a much better league. They did not think Cleveland stood a chance against NFL teams. The Browns set out to prove them wrong!

Their first game was against the Philadelphia Eagles. The Eagles were the defending NFL champions. Everyone expected a blowout game. It was—for the Browns! They pounded the Eagles, 35-10. The Browns only lost two games that season. At playoff time, they took home the NFL championship. Now, everyone knew Cleveland could play with the best.

## Chapter 2
# Browns All-Time Greats

The first Browns' teams had a powerhouse offense. Quarterback Otto Graham was at the heart of it. Coach Paul Brown had seen Graham play in college. He thought he was fantastic! Graham was the first player Brown hired. Graham played with Cleveland for the next ten years. His nickname was "Automatic Otto." That was because his passing was so **reliable**.

*Otto Graham and Paul Brown*

*Brown escapes from a Giants tackler.*

Running back Jim Brown came on board in 1957. He was fast, but also big. Opponents had a hard time stopping him. One said it was like running into a tree! Brown played nine NFL seasons. He was the NFL rushing champ in eight of them!

In 2020, the NFL turned 100 years old. It picked an all-time team. Brown was an easy pick as one of the running backs.

Quarterback Brian Sipe led the Browns in 1979 and 1980. He could pull out last-minute wins. In 1979, the Browns were losing to the Kansas City Chiefs. There was less than a minute left. Sipe threw to wide receiver Reggie Rucker for the winning touchdown. A few weeks later the Browns faced the Miami Dolphins. The game went to **overtime**. Sipe passed 39 yards to Rucker. Another touchdown . . . another win!

Clay Matthews joined the Browns in 1978. The linebacker was a rock on Cleveland's defense. He led the NFL in tackles for many years. He played 232 games in 16 years. That is a long career for a linebacker!

Tight end Ozzie Newsome also was a star player. Bulky linebackers were too slow to stop him. Safeties and **cornerbacks** were too small to stop him. Newsome is the team's all-time leader in catches.

*Ozzie Newsome*

**FUN FACT**
Brian Sipe led the NFL with 28 TD passes in 1979.

Some of Cleveland's best players are from recent seasons. Wide receiver Josh Cribbs came to Cleveland in 2005. He was especially good at kickoff returns. It is very hard to score a touchdown from a kickoff. Cribbs did it eight times in his career. In a 2009 game against the Kansas City Chiefs, he did it twice!

Joe Thomas played offensive tackle for the Browns from 2007-2017. He played every single snap of every game for his whole career. That was 10,363 snaps in a row! That is an NFL record.

*Joe Thomas*

# BROWNS RECORDS

These players piled up the best stats in Browns history. The numbers are career records through the 2019 season.

**Total TDs:** Jim Brown, 126

**TD Passes:** Brian Sipe, 154

**Passing Yards:** Brian Sipe, 23,713

**Rushing Yards:** Jim Brown, 12,312

**Receptions:** Ozzie Newsome, 662

**Points:** Lou Groza, 1,608

**Sacks:** Clay Matthews, 62

## Chapter 3
# Browns Superstars

Watching the Browns play today means watching some great talent. Quarterback Baker Mayfield played baseball and football in high school. He chose to play football in college. Good choice! He was the very first player chosen in the 2018 **NFL Draft**.

Three games into the 2018 season, the Browns were playing the New York Jets. The Browns were in trouble. They were down 14-0 and their QB got hurt. Mayfield had to go in. Could he turn it around? He did! He passed for more than 200 yards and led the Browns to their first win of the season.

Baker is a great athlete. In 2019, he ran for three touchdowns.

Baker Mayfield

Nick Chubb

When Mayfield throws, wide receiver Jarvis Landry is often there to catch it. Landry started his career with the Miami Dolphins. The Browns traded for him in 2018. Another good move! That year, Landry led the team in catches.

Running back Nick Chubb is one of the NFL's best. He often racks up more than 100 yards per game. In 2018, he ran 92 yards to score a touchdown against the Atlanta Falcons. That was the longest rushing TD in the Browns' history. Chubb rushed 20 times in a 2019 game against the Baltimore Ravens. He made three touchdowns and sealed the Browns' win! Rushing 1,000 yards in a season is another big accomplishment. In 2019, Chubb hit that mark before anyone else in the NFL.

Jarvis Landry

*Denzel Ward makes a solid tackle.*

On defense, the Browns rely on cornerback Denzel Ward. Ward says his father told him to "make people know his name." Ward joined the Browns in 2018. He racked up the tackles and **interceptions**. He also went to the Pro Bowl. In a 2019 game against the Cincinnati Bengals, he intercepted the ball. Then he ran 61 yards for a touchdown. Everyone knew his name!

Defensive end Sheldon Richardson has played for several NFL teams. He landed with the Browns for the 2019 season. Richardson is very flexible. He can step into all kinds of different situations. That makes the defense even stronger.

The Browns have a long history. They have a long list of talented players. Now they want to go to the Super Bowl. They hope that will *not* be much longer!

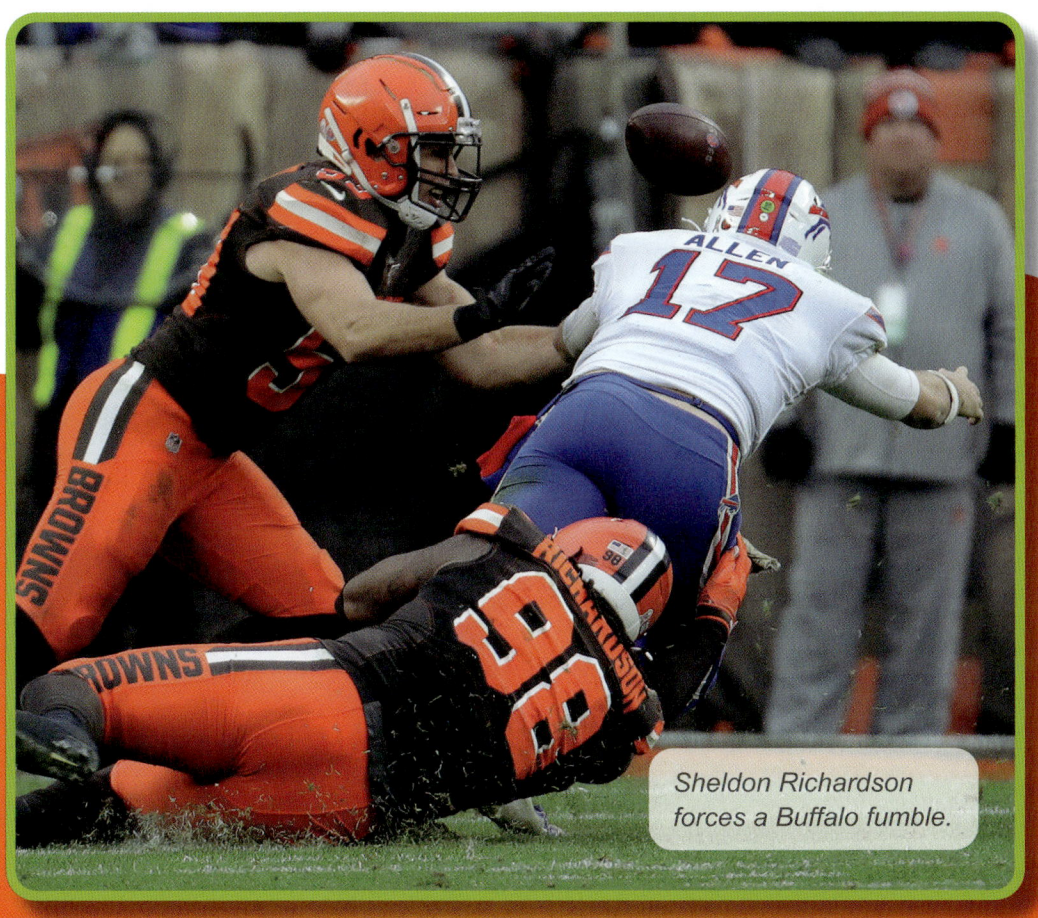

Sheldon Richardson forces a Buffalo fumble.

# BEYOND THE BOOK

After reading the book, it's time to think about what you learned. Try the following exercises to jumpstart your ideas.

## RESEARCH

**FIND OUT MORE.** Where would you go to find out more about your favorite NFL teams and players? Check out NFL.com, of course. Each team also has its own website. What other sports information sites can you find? See if you can find other cool facts about your favorite team.

## CREATE

**GET ARTISTIC.** Each NFL team has a logo. The Browns don't really have a logo! Get some art materials and try designing your own Browns logo. Or create a new team and make a logo for it. What colors would you choose? How would you draw the mascot?

## DISCOVER

**GO DEEP!** As this book shows, the Browns have really struggled in recent seasons. What would you say to Browns fans to keep them excited? How do you think losing so much affects the players? Read about other teams that have lost a lot and see what you can discover.

## GROW

**GET OUT AND PLAY!** You don't need to be in the NFL to enjoy football. You just need a football and some friends. Play touch or tag football. Or you can hang cloth flags from your belt; grab the belt and make the "tackle." See who has the best arm to be quarterback. Who is the best receiver? Who can run the fastest? Time to play football!

# RESEARCH NINJA

Visit www.ninjaresearcher.com/2251 to learn how to take your research skills and book report writing to the next level!

## RESEARCH

**DIGITAL LITERACY TOOLS**

**SEARCH LIKE A PRO**
Learn about how to use search engines to find useful websites.

**FACT OR FAKE?**
Discover how you can tell a trusted website from an untrustworthy resource.

**TEXT DETECTIVE**
Explore how to zero in on the information you need most.

**SHOW YOUR WORK**
Research responsibly—learn how to cite sources.

## WRITE

**GET TO THE POINT**
Learn how to express your main ideas.

**PLAN OF ATTACK**
Learn prewriting exercises and create an outline.

**DOWNLOADABLE REPORT FORMS**

# Further Resources

## BOOKS

Fishman, Jon. *Baker Mayfield (Sports All-Stars)*. Minneapolis: Lerner Books, 2020.

*Football: Then to Wow!* New York: Sports Illustrated Kids, 2014.

Whiting, Jim. *Cleveland Browns (NFL Today)*. Minneapolis: Creative Education, 2019.

## WEBSITES

**FACTSURFER**

Factsurfer.com gives you a safe, fun way to find more information.

1. Go to www.factsurfer.com.
2. Enter "Cleveland Browns" into the search box and click 🔍
3. Select your book cover to see a list of related websites.

# Glossary

**blowout:** a game in which one team scores a lot more than the other. Cleveland's 50–0 score made their win a blowout.

**cornerback:** a defensive position that covers receivers. The cornerback was so close to the receiver that he could not make the catch.

**interceptions:** passes caught by the defense. Interceptions are a quarterback's least favorite kind of pass.

**loyal:** able to keep supporting something no matter what. Browns fans stick with their team; they are very loyal.

**NFL Draft:** the annual event at which NFL teams choose college players. Cleveland's first pick in the 2020 NFL Draft was tackle Jedrick Wills.

**overtime:** extra time added when a 60-minute game ends in a tie. Cleveland tied the game 10–10 and then won 13–10 in overtime.

**reliable:** always ready to do the job. Browns fans could trust Joe Thomas to be reliable.

**rivals:** fierce opponents. Cincinnati is Cleveland's biggest NFL rival.

**rookie:** a player in his or her first pro season. In 2020, Cleveland's top rookie was lineback Mack Wilson.

# Index

All-America Football Conference, 6, 8, 15
Atlanta Falcons, 25
Baltimore Colts, 8
Baltimore Ravens, 25
Brown, Jim, 17
Brown, Paul, 6, 16
Chubb, Nick, 25
Cincinnati Bengals, 26
Cribbs, Josh, 20
"Dawg Pound," 5
Graham, Otto, 6, 16
Groza, Lou, 8
Kansas City Chiefs, 18, 20
Landry, Jarvis, 25
Lavelli, Dante, 6
Los Angeles Rams, 8
Matthews, Clay, 18
Mayfield, Baker, 22, 25
Miami Dolphins, 18, 25
Motley, Marion, 6
move to Baltimore, 10
New York Jets, 22
Newsom, Ozzie, 18
Philadelphia Eagles, 15
Pittsburgh Steelers, 9
Richardson, Sheldon, 27
Rucker, Reggie, 18
San Francisco 49ers, 8
Sipe, Brian, 18
Thomas, Joe, 20
Ward, Denzel, 26
Willis, Bill, 6

## PHOTO CREDITS

The images in this book are reproduced through the courtesy of: AP Images: Tony Dejak 4; PFHOF 6; Tony Tomsic 8, 9, 18; Roberto Borea 10; David Richard 12; Julian C. Wilson 14; 16, 17; Peter Read Miller 19. Focus on Football: 22, 23, 24, 25. Newscom: Paul Tople/KRT 11; Phil Masturzo/TNS 20, 27; Frank Jansky/Icon SW 26. **Cover photo:** Focus on Football.

# About the Author

Diane Bailey has written dozens of books for kids and teens, on everything from sports to science to civil rights. She has two grown sons and lives with her husband in Kansas, where they like to watch football, talk about football, argue about football, and look forward to more football!